for Marco
Keep writing
Lynn
4/14.

Learning to Say "Sátoraljaújhely"

finding a place in a Hungarian Jewish family

Lynn Saul

Jumping
Cholla
Press

Tucson Arizona

Library of Congress Control Number: 2010908232

1. Fiction   2. Poetry 3.   Essays 4. Jews—Hungary—History.

Cover photograph: Tent Mountain, Sátoraljaújhely, Lynn Saul, 2004

ISBN 978-1-884106-09-5

2010

Jumping
Cholla
Press

Jumping Cholla Press
P. O. Box 2572
Tucson Arizona 85702

Learning to Say "Sátoraljaújhely"

Grateful acknowledgment is made to the editors of the following journals, where some of the poems, stories, and personal essays in this collection first appeared:

Jewish Women's Literary Annual: "Mythology in Three Parts"
SandScript: "At Héviz," "Learning to Say 'Sátoraljaújhely'"
ShalomVeg: "The Gardens"

to the Tucson Jewish Community Center and Central Arizona College, Aravaipa for exhibits of some of these and others of my photographs of Hungary

and many thanks also to the Tucson/Pima Arts Council for a generous grant to fund my travel to participate in the Hungarian Multicultural Center artists' residency in Balatonfüred, 2004

and to the Hungarian Multicultural Center and Beata Szechy for a transformative experience

In memory of my mother, Ruth Friedman Saul, who first took me to Hungary, and my grandfather, Nicholas J. Friedman, who told us his story on tape.

ז״ל

5

CONTENTS

Count Vaj's castle, on road to Poroskő, 1997

Birth record of Miksa (Nicholas) Friedman, entry #59, (born November 9, 1889) Sátoraljaújhely archives, 1997

Marriage record of Wolf Friedman and Rezi Perlstein, entry #20, Sátoraljaújhely archives, 1997. Married July 14, 1886.

Right side of marriage record of Wolf Friedman and Rezi Perlstein, listing David Reichard and Jakab Schlanger as witnesses, Sátoraljaújhely archives, 1997

WHAT I'M HOPING TO FIND

Lynn, 1997

Why are you going to Hungary? he asks me.
What do you hope to find? Tell me,
What would it take to make you happy?
For your ancestors to sit up in their graves
and tell you how it really was? I guess,
I stammer, that's what I want
but since they won't, I want
the next best thing: finding
their stories on carved stone
and archived in small print.
Name of midwife: Friedman Re'zi
Name of circumciser: Bermann Lipot
Name of godfather: Reichard David, wine trader.
Was the midwife an aunt? Was she trained
or merely the sister-in-law
trying to help—
or to control?
Was the godfather, the wine merchant,
a friend of the gambling father
who came to America to avoid his debts?
What did the house at Kazinczy Utca 515
look like? What sort of people would
have lived there? I'm looking for the rest
of the stories I know:
the exposition, the prequel. Yes, I tell him,
I want them to sit up in their graves
and tell me
my truth.

Fani Schoenberger Friedman Schlanger. Photo by Elvira Photostudio, Varanno. No date.

GRANDMA FRIEDMAN

Fani Schoenberger Friedman Schlanger, Poroskő, 1894

I feel like such a grown up. I never expected this, to be a matron. Part of me, especially at night when dreams come, still feels like that young girl who spent hours along the river, even wading in, even swimming downstream and walking back through the willow thickets, stopping to sit on the boulders along the shore to dry my dress and my hair in the sun before I went back home to my mother, who had no idea what I'd been doing.

After Shmule died, of course, I took to wearing black. I've decided I like it, the way the black cloth sets off my olive skin.

When I was in Varanno last month, visiting my sister and her family, they got me to stop at the photographer's studio and sit for a portrait. I remember my mother saying that the camera would capture your *neshama* and not to do it. My father would just mumble something about the second commandment. No graven images. But this isn't like that. It's not a statue or an expensive painting. And I can send it to my son who lives in New York now. I don't know when I'll see him, or the boys, again.

I'm carrying my parasol. It was a hot June day when we went to the studio. I remembered being a young girl, wearing thin white cotton dresses, gathering flowers along the river to weave into my hair. There was a woman in our village who did beautiful embroidery. Once my father bought one of her embroidered dresses to give me as a Shabbos present. I must have been seven or eight years old. It was the most beautiful dress I've ever seen. Around the neck, and at the wrists, and along the hem of the skirt were flowers, bright red and yellow with green twirling leaves, blooming like my mother's garden in June.

Last night I dreamed that Wolf and Rezi had come back home, with their boys and with a beautiful baby girl. Rezi looked so beautiful, cradling

13

the baby in her arms, wrapped in a white crocheted blanket. When the little girl would be a few years older, I would get her a dress like the one my father got for me. I would take her to the photographer's studio and have her portrait made so that she would always be able to see how beautiful she is, but then I would tell her to take the dress off and put it away carefully and dress in ordinary clothes and then I would take her down to the river and teach her how to swim.

THE GARDENS

In Poroskő my ancestors were tenant farmers
hired other laborers to work the fields
which Jews were not allowed to own

Wheat, cabbages, corn perhaps
They had orchards of plums
peaches, apples

Always the flowers
four-o-clocks
daisies
clematis
wild blooms

in well-kept rows
the green effusion
of grape leaves

Along the river and in every yard
grew willows
Even on the gravestones
graceful willows
watered like the Tree of Life
promised a rooted soul

Poroskő 1997

Lynn at Friedman Family Cemetery, Poroskő 1997

"BIG STRAPPING HUNGARIAN WOMAN"

Hani Czinner Perlstein, Sátoraljaújhely, 1910, speaking to Lynn, 2010

You don't know me...

A voice has been whispering in my ear. First quietly. In the middle of the night. Then when I'm staring at the computer screen. When I lean back in my chair and listen to music. A rhythmic, lyrical sound. The violins.

You don't know me. But I recognize you.

I'm Hungarian, like all that music you're listening to—Magyar. Magyar Zsidó, like you. But I do have red hair, like your mother. Yes, your mother told you that redheads are really Egyptian. Well, we were all in Egypt. Mitzraim, remember. Who knows, our genes have been mixed up for a long time. But I'm as Hungarian as they come, Hungarian and Jewish. Magyar Zsidó.

Maybe it's that distant Egyptian that makes me stand tall and proud. But we Hungarians are proud, too. Why not? We've got a beautiful country and a beautiful life. Oh, Lynn, how you'd love the forests here, and the gardens. Well, yes, I remember that you visited briefly and saw for yourself. But to see them all the time, in all seasons.... The gardens are like Gan Eden, you know. Full of golden apricots and purple grapes and blushing apples and soft green pears. Sunflowers and strawberries. We walk in the woods full of mushrooms, gather them in baskets. A good life, Lynn, one you'd love.

I'm not like your Aunt Enny. She's a little stuck up, I'm afraid. She married that lawyer and thinks she's better than some people. All she wears is silk and fine linen, hand embroidered. I still dig in the dirt...

That's not fair. I've seen Enny's garden. She has gotten her hands in the dirt, but I know she cared about fine handmade lingerie...

There you go. Well, maybe I'm being unfair. She's my granddaughter, she was named for me, and I must be a little disappointed in her, I guess. But we'll leave her out of this. I'll just tell you about me. It's my story I want you to tell.

My name is Hani. I was born in Sátoraljaújhely in 1844, or maybe it was earlier, 1842, just before the Revolution that was largely invented there. My father was Elias, part of the large Czinner family that has always been important in Újhely. My mother's name was Fani, but I never learned what her own family name was. She died and I named a daughter after her in 1868, but my daughter was mostly known as Ervin.

After the Revolution, which failed so quickly, it was very important to think of ourselves as Hungarian.

After the failed 1848 revolution! This is the period of the crackdown against Hungarian nationalism, the absolutist period, when the Austro-Hungarian (Austrian) government insisted on the use of German in the schools, forbade the teaching of Hungarian history.... So it is a statement of being Hungarian rather than Austrian! It is a statement of language choice of Hungarian not only against Yiddish but against German. It is a statement of belief in democracy and self-determination as against the imperialistic and absolutist Habsburg government.

Lynn, your grandfather described me to you as a "big strapping Hungarian woman," and that is what I was. I was Hungarian. When I went to school, they tried to keep us from speaking Hungarian at school. We had to speak German. They tried not to teach us Hungarian history. I remember how my teachers would go into the hallway and look around, then come back into the classroom and begin to talk about ....

SZÓDAVÍZ

Hani Czinner Perlstein, Sátoraljaújhely, 1890

After the champion billiards player in Hungary died, leaving me with my four little daughters, I had the opportunity to acquire the equipment for bottling *szódavíz* and a donkey and a little wagon for hauling the zinc-topped bottles around. Customers were not a problem. Everyone wanted some of the fizzy clear liquid, and my brother the druggist insisted that there was sure to be a cure in every glass, or at least a preventative. As soon as the girls left for school every morning, I would fill ten bottles, place them carefully in a wooden crate, and place the crate on the wagon, do the same thing several more times, hitch the donkey to the wagon, and set off up and down the hilly streets of Újhely, delivering one or two bottles to various houses, and six or eight to several of the taverns and csárdas with whom I'd obtained regular contracts.

It was good exercise to walk alongside my donkey, Számla, and if I had no time to chat with my friends, at least we could exchange a smile and "*Jó reggelt, kívánok*" or "*csókolom*" as I went on my way. Sometimes one of my acquaintances, seeing what merchandise I carried, would ask for details, take a bottle on trial, and by the next week return it empty and request a regular delivery.

Sometimes as Számla and I climbed the cobblestone streets that led up through the vineyards on the slopes of Kis-szár-hegy, I wondered how Emanuel Perlstein had gone so far from our childhood days when he'd been an ordinary Jewish boy who had a predictable future in a trade or perhaps as a traveling salesman, but instead he found himself more and more playing billiards, first in taverns and then in the casinos of Sátoraljaújhely, and when we were married his father promised my father that he really was becoming an excellent salesman, that he made friends easily wherever he went, and could travel from Újhely to Ungvar and Vinograd and Munkacs and Miskolc and Mad without fear and even without attracting trouble, and he always brought back new items to sell that were more interesting than the ones he'd started with at the beginning of a trip, and his father promised my father that the billiards was a bachelor's pastime only and that when he was married, of course Emanuel would be home each *Shabbos* and *Yom Tov* and even some weekdays, because he would make so much money on each trip that he would not need to travel constantly.

Mani used to say that when he was running a table, he felt completely alive. Each time the cue stick hit a ball, the sharp sound, as perfectly in pitch as a properly bowed string, woke up something in his head, like the perfect ray of sunlight on a fan of chestnut leaves. When he heard that sound, he knew everything in his life had fallen into place—he would win the game, he would make money that night, he would sell a lot of merchandise the next day, he would come home to our perfect house, to my perfectly set *Shabbos* table, he would kiss each of his perfectly beautiful daughters, he would eat my perfectly cooked *ponty*, he would make love to me on *Shabbos* night with the perfect timing of a billiards game. That's what he would say.

After Mani gave up selling and started spending his days and his nights playing billiards in Nyíregyháza and Debrecen, he would come home on *Shabbos* and, when we were lying under the goose-down cover, he would say that when he was running a table, he would feel the numbers in his head, that it was a precise arithmetic, *a számtan*, more elegant than anything he had learned in school or seen diagrammed by his brother, who had become an arithmetic teacher. It was not simply the number of balls and pockets, he would say. There was a certain geometry, but it was never calculated in advance. It was a perfect pattern that, he said, formed in his head and then slipped into his arms and then to the ball, and he said it was the way he felt now, and softly placed his hands on my shoulders and moved them down my arms with a gentle sureness that did feel mathematical, although, of course, I had never studied mathematics, but for a moment I understood what Mani was trying to explain to me.

And now, even though I walk up and down the streets and am tired at the end of each day, and even though I do not have the life I had been promised, it's that geometry I remember, the perfect order that Mani gave to me that was never calculated in advance.

Szódavíz, Balatonfüred 2004

Hani Czinner Perlstein Reichard

Sátoraljaújhely, no date

CATTLE KILLING, PART I

(transcript of Nicholas Friedman tape, talking about his father Wolf's brothers, in Poroskő)

Then these brothers started fightin' each other...they'd get jealous and fightin'...one brother'd go and cut the throat of five or six of the cattle, you know, and they had lawsuits and fightin' around, till they'd lost almost everything.

CATTLE KILLING, PART II

Wolf Friedman, Porosků, 1875; Lynn, Tohono O'Odham Nation in Arizona, 1985

Wolf's great-granddaughter is lying in bed in her trailer on the Tohono O'Odham Nation in Southern Arizona. Dreams floating through her head, floating and disappearing. Outside her bedroom window, a large mesquite tree shades this room as well as the small chicken coop whose residents wake her up every morning. Someone was banging on her front door.

She'd moved here to change things that weren't working in her life—a battle with her ex-husband she was tired of fighting, frustrations with her law practice. She'd hoped to fill her need for a quiet life where she could devote herself to her writing. She took a job as a legal services lawyer that would pay her a salary for no more than 40 hours of work each week and tried to learn a new way to communicate, without the verbalization she'd excelled in naturally, an inherent part of her cultures—Jewish, academic, legal. The Tohono O'Odham were reputedly a silent people, a culture of few words...

But the O'Odham weren't such a quiet people after all. They were the most social people Wolf's great-granddaughter had ever been among. That first week, four or five feasts—All Souls, private memorial dinners, a dinner in honor of a man in her office who had been appointed as a judge. And always all-night chicken-scratch dances and parties and even wakes—people not at all quiet and shy, only around outsiders did they seem that way. But they didn't talk just to talk.

The loud banging on the trailer door woke them both up, Wolf's great-granddaughter and the O'Odham man lying next to her in bed. A voice outside the door was yelling his name. "Hu:si, Hu:si," and he jumped out of bed and came back a moment later to tell the startled, groggy figure half-sitting on the edge of the bed, "Snake needs me to go help him over at the Livestock Complex." She looked at the digital alarm on the dresser. 2:45 am.

It was nearly dawn when Hu:si got back and began to tell Wolf's great-granddaughter the story that finished the one her grandfather, Wolf's son, had told her years earlier. Living here on the Arizona-Mexico border, in a community of small-scale cattle ranchers, the story about brothers killing each others' cows in Ung Megye, Hungary a century earlier, began to make sense.

THE CARD PLAYER

Wolf Friedman, Poroskő, 1884; Sátoraljaújhely, 1893

"I've bought a ticket to New York. I'm leaving at the end of the week."

"Leaving? But, Wolf, the baby will be due very soon."

"I can't stay. They're after me now. They'll come and take everything we have. You can stay with your mother."

Rezi put her hands on the lace tablecloth that had been a wedding present. "You can't go now. They'll come after us here. They'll take everything. Sandor will be so embarassed at school."

"No, you don't need me to be here. Your mother has engaged the midwife, she has arranged a tutor for Sandor, she has hired a nurse for Miksa.... She has taken care of everything. You'll go to her. After I'm settled in New York, I'll send you steamship tickets."

"Oh, Wolf, I am so afraid. You will be so far away. You won't even know...."

I poured a glass of brandy from the crystal decanter. "Rezi, I love you but I've made some mistakes. I wanted to fit in with your family. I love playing cards with your stepfather's friends, the way they talk, hearing about the places they've been."

I remembered the days just before I left Poroskő to come to Újhely. I was in the back of the house when I heard the horses braying, the men shouting. I ran into the front room, and through the open door I could see the infamous Vaj and his men on black horses, riding right up to the door. My mother, a stocky woman who even now could get me to do anything she ordered, straightened her black dress and opened the door.

"We demand the presence of all the sons of Samuel Friedman."

They were thin, mustached men in fur-collared coats, each astride a black horse with silver medallions on the bridles.

"Only the youngest are here, David and Wolf," Mother said.

"We know there are more. We must have them all at once, all eight. And David and Wolf are not so young, we know that," Vaj snapped.

"What do you want them for? We are poor Jews..."

"You are irresponsible tenants on our land. Criminals. My deputies have found at least ten dead cows, their throats slashed, their carcasses left to rot, not even good for meat. This is our land."

I watched Mother's shoulders droop, her black dress falling in folds over her ample chest. Vaj hadn't seen me yet, and I couldn't decide if I wanted to go out into the yard and confront him myself, or if I was willing to let Mother handle the problem. But I knew I couldn't stay in Poroskő any longer. Vaj had ruined the lives of those Jewish timber workers from Tiszaeszlár last year, charging them with that ridiculous but historic crime they always try to bring against us Jews, "ritual murder," after those men had found a dead girl floating in the Tisza river while they were taking logs to market. I'd go off to see our cousin Karoly in Nyíregyháza. He'd gotten them off, he could help us.

Mother came back inside and slammed the door shut. "Mother," I said.

"Shhhh," she said. "They'll hear you. They want you."

"I know," I said. "I'm going to leave. I'll go to see Karoly. He'll be able to help."

"You're a good son, Wolf," she said, pulling the drapes closed over the window. "I know you want to help us. I know you wouldn't do anything wrong. I'm not so sure about Yitz or Feri. They're crazy sometimes. They've been spending too much time at Gusti's tavern."

"It's hard for so many of us to live here. There's only so much land, and we have more cows than it can really support. But Jews can't buy land, and Vaj will only rent us so much." I said. "But they both love you, and they feel like they've had to take care of you since Father died."

"Well, I can take care of myself. And I'm going to get married again, actually."

"Married? Who are you planning to marry?" I asked her. This certainly would complicate my plans.

"Yakov Schlanger is a good man, and he has enough money to help us invest in the farm. I think we'll get married before Passover."

I tried to imagine my mother as Schlanger Jakabné. She'd been running the farm herself for ten years now, and doing a damn good job. What did she want now, to become a society wife and have the neighbors in for tea? Schlanger had money all right, but I couldn't see him as a farmer.

When I came to Újhely, I went to see David Reichard, a wine merchant my new stepfather had done business with for many years. Jakab Schlanger let me know that he'd written to Reichard about me, that he was sure he could help set me up in business.

"You think you would like to deal with men's clothing, a haberdashery?" Reichard had asked me when I went to see him in his cellars. He was a tall, very handsome man. He had the air of someone who had traveled, who knew something of what I wanted to learn about the world. "There's a shop for let on the side street, around the corner from the town hall. It's a good location and you could do very well there. By the way, do you play cards?"

"I do, sir," I said.

"Well, a group of us will be meeting at the Tent Mountain Casino this evening. All fine Jewish men, in business, they can be helpful to you, and a charming evening besides. Please come at eight."

I knew I had made the right decision to come here to Újhely, although I missed the rolling hills above the Ung valley at Poroskő. Reichard and I arranged to go together to look at the shop the next morning, and I went back to my room to unpack and get ready for an evening of cards. Perhaps I would even win enough to increase the initial stock I could carry.

I played cards that night, and after seeing the shop the next day, took it and within a few weeks had opened Friedman's Haberdashery. Reichard was a faithful mentor, introducing me to jobbers from Vienna who could provide me with fine linen shirts and silk ties made in Paris. I sent some of my profits to cousin Karoly to represent my reckless brothers in the lawsuit Vaj had brought to oust them from the farm, and invested my gambling winnings in stocking more sophisticated merchandise at the store. Some of the men let me borrow when the cards weren't coming right, because they seemed to enjoy my company. Then, one evening at the casino, Reichard suggested that I come to his home on Sunday afternoon for tea. "My wife has a daughter who is old enough to marry. I think you would find her attractive and suitable," he said as he handed me a whiskey.

Rezi Perlstein was the most beautiful woman I had ever seen. Her fine auburn hair was pulled into a soft bun at the back of her hair. Her eyes were soft, her skin lightly freckled—she wasn't afraid to go out into the sun, I could see. She wore a high-necked, precisely tucked silk waist in a pale lavender color that perfectly set off her light brown eyes. Her earrings were delicate pearl and gold. We were married on July 14, 1886. Rezi gave birth to two fine sons, I did well in the store, and for awhile I did well at cards.

"I don't want to go to New York," Rezi said. She stood up and walked out the door into the courtyard. The grapevines were lush, huge fresh green leaves covering the back porch. The Holland tulips she'd planted in the fall were still in bloom, bright red punctuating the deep brown flowerbeds. Over the wall she could see the tall blunt shape of Tent Mountain, covered with green grapevines. I followed her outside, put my hand on her shoulder.

Then I turned and went back into the house, into the bedroom.   I pulled the leather valise down from the shelf, opened it, and turned to take the starched white collars out of my drawer.

July 15, 1997. Wolf and Rezi's granddaughter, Ruth, and her daughters, search in the archives of the Sátoraljaújhely Town Hall for traces of their ancestors:

> NAMELESS, born July 22, 1893, a boy, to Friedman Vilmos merchant the younger and Perlstein Rezi of Sátoraljaújhely. Midwife Friedman Abrahamne. Died before circumcision, July 31. Note: "his father has emigrated to America."

Wolf Friedman serving in military, probably a few years before his marriage to Rezi

Four ladies, unidentified, probably Rezi Perlstein and her sisters, Sátoraljaújhely, no date

REZI

Rezi Perlstein Friedman, Sátoraljaújhely, 1893

After the baby died, they made me stay in bed for six weeks. They didn't even have a funeral, of course, the baby was too sick even to have a bris, so he didn't have a name, didn't even count as a life. We didn't sit shiva, nobody came to the house, and besides, there I was again at my mother's house, or rather, at my stepfather's house, because his house was so much nicer and we'd moved in there the day my mother married him. I moved back into my old room at the front of the house, and they drew the heavy green velvet drapes closed because sun wasn't supposed to be good for me, and Mama and Margit did everything they could to keep Sandor and Miksa out of my way, or even to know what was going on. But of course every day they asked where Papa was and Sandor especially kept asking when we'd go to America to be with him. Margit would shush him and tell him I needed my rest, and then she would take the boys by the hand and close the tall double cherrywood doors behind her, leaving me alone in this dark cave of a room. The only thing I liked about the room was the photograph of Queen Maria Theresa that hung on the wall next to the window. She was so beautiful, and I had been named for her, *Rezi*, like so many other Hungarian girls, especially Hungarian Jewish girls like me, because supposedly she had given so many rights to the Jews. *You're as beautiful as a princess*, my mother always told me, and my stepfather actually expected people to treat me that way.

Every morning, my mother would come into my room, bring warm water and help me wash, and bring me sage tea and warm bread and currant jam. "This will help you heal," she would say, and then, when I had finished my breakfast, she would take the tray away and tell me to rest again.

In the afternoon, Dr. Friedman came by, the midwife's husband, a tall man with gold spectacles and a large leather valise full of strange tools that he didn't use on me. He only sat in the high-backed armchair which he pulled up next to the bed and sipped tea while he asked me whether I felt any stronger. "Please, can you open the draperies," I would ask him. "You are not yet strong enough," he said, and then he would leave.

Finally, one afternoon, he said, yes, we should open the draperies, and in fact, he thought it would be good for me to take dinner with the family in the dining room. Margit was with us in my room when he said that, and she turned to me, her eyes smiling for the first time since the baby had been born and died, and she held out her hands to help me out of bed. "Let me get a fresh gown for you to put on, Rezi," she said. After she helped me dress, she brushed my hair and tied it back for me with a spray of flowers from the garden. "You look like a girl, not an old married lady!" she said, handing me the glass to see myself for the first time in weeks. Then she pulled open the drapes, and I looked out the window into the courtyard, full of late summer flowers, and the first few strands of red paprika hanging from the eaves.

"Oh, Mama, good evening, it is so good that you are joining us for dinner," Sandor announced when I sat down at the table. He sat tall in the chair next to me, and little Miksa came over and gave me a kiss before going back into the kitchen with the maid. "Don't get up, please," my stepfather said as he came into the room. "Please, Rezi, we are so glad you are able to be here with us again. We will invite Wolf's mother to visit next week, since you are looking so well. But you will have to cover your hair if she is going to be here."

"Yes, be a proper married lady again," Margit said, smiling at me. It was wonderful to see my sister smiling again, laughing.

All I could eat that night was a small piece of fish and a little bread, but I was glad to be with people again, and dressed in nice clothes. In the next few weeks, before it became cold, I would go for short walks with Margit. Mother Friedman never did come to visit, so I almost felt like a young girl again, just as Margit had suggested, but I thought of Wolf all

34

the time, wishing that he were not so far away, wishing that we had not had to give up our house, wishing that I did not have to look the other way when I walked in the market square.

One afternoon, when Margit and I were walking, she turned to me and stopped. "You know, Rezi," she said, "you could get a divorce from Wolf if you wanted to."

I stopped and stared at her. I couldn't think of anything to say.

"He gambled all your money away. He's an embarrassment to the Reichard family. He had to leave the country in such a hurry. And couldn't even stay here while you had the baby. That's probably the reason the baby died. The Rabbi will make him grant you a divorce. He made Weiss give one to Eszti, you know."

"No, Margit, I don't want to be divorced. I love Wolf, even though I know it's been hard. You don't understand. Remember where he came from, the farm, and all those problems with his brothers. He didn't mean to lose so much money. He was just trying to make a better life for us, and it wasn't working. He thinks things will be better in New York."

"Are you really planning to take the boys and go to America?" Margit asked me, as though this was the first time she'd heard the idea. "I would miss all of you so much! And I've heard that it's hard there. No one has maids, you have to do all the cooking and cleaning yourself. You don't speak English or Yiddish. Nobody in New York knows Hungarian. What would you do?"

"Wolf will take care of us. He's already learning English, according to his letter. He wrote that he's buying a store there. He's going to send us steamship tickets as soon as I'm well enough to travel. But I really will miss you, Margit, you know that. And Mama and Father also. Perhaps in a few years we'll be able to come back, all of us. That's what I'd really like, for it to be the way it was until now. Our own house, our own garden, afternoons when the four of us sat in the garden together and Wolf and I watched the boys playing...."

"You've walked far enough for today," Margit said, and turned around to return home. I stopped to look around the square before catching up with her. The beautiful yellow stucco on the City Hall building had taken on tints of orange from the almost-setting sun. The geraniums hanging from the second-story windows were still bright red. I decided to stop at the book seller's stand to look for a new volume of poetry before returning home, and I called out for Margit to wait for me. Sure enough, she found me a copy of Ormódy's book, a Jewish Hungarian poet to remind me why I should stay here.

"Thank you," I said as she paid for the book for me.

"A get-well present," she smiled.

Rezi Perlstein Friedman, no date

A FENCE AROUND KOLOSVAR, A FENCE AROUND ÚJHELY

Rezi Perlstein Friedman, Brooklyn, New York, 1895

My chest feels so tight. Each breath I try to take is conscious, an effort: I must do this. I feel how small my chest is. Like taking tiny steps on an icy road. Making sure there will be a next step, a next breath. I am exhausted from the effort. My eyelids close, but I am afraid to close my eyes, to sleep, for then I may cease these small breaths.

This room is so small, so unlike our house in Újhely, so unlike the room in my mother's house where I stayed after Wolf left for New York. There are no French doors opening on a garden. There are no heavy velvet drapes to keep out the sun, but there is no sun. Just a small window hung with thin curtains, looking out on the grimy walls of the house across the street, the grimy gray air of Brooklyn, the clatter of the street car, the shouts of the children playing stickball on the sidewalk.

Under the window is a small bureau, the only furniture we brought from home. Wolf arranged to have it shipped here when I came last year with the boys. There's a lace runner on top of it that my mother had given me, and a silver mirror and comb and brush set that my stepfather gave me before I left. I don't have the strength to brush my own hair. Mrs. Goldstein from across the hall comes in every morning and brushes it for me. "Such a beautiful mirror," she says every time, holding it up for me to see how she has brushed back the thinning strands of mousy brown hair and pulled them into a small bun at my neck. "You have beautiful things," she says, "so nice that you were able to bring them with you." She sighs, goes into the next room for a few minutes, and returns with a tray of a teapot and cup, and a slice of toast. She places the tray on the bureau and pulls back the curtain. "It's going to be a hot day," she says. She pours me a cup of tea and brings the cup to my lips. "Drink a little of this," she says. "It will make it easier for you." I try to sip the tea, and I can feel its heat sliding into my chest. My eyelids begin to close and I hear the cup clink back onto the saucer. "Köszönöm," I mutter, but Mrs. Goldstein doesn't understand me. She sits on a chair next to my bed, though, her cool hand around mine.

In my dream I can breathe. In my dream I am taking a long walk with Wolf. Hand in hand we are walking along Kazinczy Utca in Újhely, past the bright yellow City Hall with its baskets of purple and white flowers cascading above us, past the convent wall and the iron gate of the Gimnázium, past Margit's balcony with its shuttered windows, past the new cemetery at the edge of town, the cemetery that my stepfather and his uncles worked so hard to endow, and out into the fields of wheat and sunflowers and paprika on the way to our new home. I am wearing a new yellow cotton dress, simple really, but with tucks on the bodice and a simple band of lace at the neck. I have a matching parasol to keep the sun off my face, and Wolf walks beside me, carrying baby Sandor in his arms. The baby squirms a little, but he's so happy being carried. "Sing, Mama," he says. I'm humming, and at his request I change the words that are borrowed from a favorite gypsy tune, crying that I can't go to Kolosvár, can't go to Újhely.

> Be van Kolosvár kerítve,
> Nu face bine, hejde
> Majd elmegyünk mink majd oda,
> Nu face bine.
> Dadjdadada...

> Be van Újhely kerítve,
> Nu face bine, hejde
> Majd elmegyünk mink majd oda,
> Nu face bine.
> Dadjdadada...

Wolf's face lights up to my song, and he starts to sing along.

When I wake up, Mrs. Goldstein is gone and Sandor is standing in the doorway, his books still hanging on the strap over his shoulder. "How are you, my dearest Mama?" he asks, then comes into the room and brings a cool, damp cloth to my forehead. "No, son," I say. "No, you must not come into the room." I turn my face away. I don't want him to become ill. How I wish I could sing to him.

Song translation:

There is a fence around Koloszvár, I don't feel good. Let's go there, I don't feel good. Dadjdadada....

(Rezi had family in Kolosvár but had not lived there, although she may have lived there later, after returning to Hungary from New York. She was just singing the traditional song, but for the second verse, Rezi has substituted the name of her most recent Hungarian residence, Újhely.)

MYTHOLOGY IN THREE PARTS

Lynn, Pittsburgh, 1948-1988

1. THE MUSIC BOX

It's broken and I want to fix it. I've had it since I was three and before that it was my mother's. Her favorite grandfather brought it to her from Europe, but it says "Made in Switzerland" in English on the inside of the lid.

This grandfather was always bringing my mother treasures from the nineteenth century: hand-made lace, a gold-and-silver tablecloth depicting an elaborate Eastern Orthodox wedding procession, a tiny sapphire-and-diamond ring, this music box. She keeps the lace put away in the back of some drawer, she uses the tablecloth for wedding and anniversary parties, but she gave me the ring and the music box.

When it worked the music box played *The Blue Danube Waltz* and *Lorelei*, played them on a brass cylinder dotted with tiny prick-points, which turned against fingers of steel that would lift and then fall with each note. Once there was a piece of glass fitted into the top of the box, but it's missing now, like one of the screws that held the works to the bottom of the box, and now the wood at the bottom of the box is broken too—I can't remember when that happened. Now it doesn't work at all, it must be overwound, the mainspring must be broken.

2. THE LORELEI

My mother was the one who first explained about
the *Lorelei*. I must have asked her, having heard the tune
only in the music box. The other melody, *Blue Danube Waltz*,

I'd heard in many other places. It didn't have
the mystery, the minor key.

41

                                        This was before

I'd read the *Odyssey*, before I knew
anything about women
                                        or men.

In the stories the Lorelei is a maiden
combing her wild golden hair
on a high cliff. Men on the Rhine below,
seeing her, seduced,
would wreck their boats and drown.

There are several stories. In each of them
the men are victims. In some
the Lorelei is too. The ghostly melody
is theirs, is hers.

3. THE BLUE DANUBE WALTZ

The Rhine is not a Jewish river. We
never understood virgins.

I do not try to understand the Rhine, only that once,
perhaps, William Friedman my great-grandfather

stopped to buy a music-box.
The Rhine is a river of dark spirits

he didn't need to understand.
William Friedman my great-grandfather

was a man of the Danube. The Danube
is a river of dancing. In white satin,

in velvet waistcoats, the men bowing,
the women circling beneath chandeliers

in a blazing ballroom, William Friedman,
in Budapest, in Vienna,

William Friedman waltzing.

Sandor, Miklos, Wolf Friedman, December 10, 1905.

Sandor, Enny, Miklos Friedman. No date.

Olga Frank, Erzsika Frank, Enny Friedman, dressed in gypsy costumes, Kolosvár, 1912

Olga Frank, Erzsika Frank, Enny Friedman, Kolosvár, no date. Postcard addressed to their grandmother, Reichard Davidné in Sátoraljaújhely, from "granddaughters"

THE HUNGARIAN ART BOOKS

Lynn, Arizona, 1985

I discover two extraordinary volumes in my dream,
one recent and surreal, contemporary art from Hungary,
the other a large book, filled with full-color plates
and dated nineteen fifty three, Hungarian art from that time,
hidden in a bookshop corner.

The older volume opens with a realistic still-life
of violins, but dark abstract-expressionist landscapes
dominate and lead me to recall
the stories my grandfather and mother told me
about our Hungarian relatives. Uncle with a timber business in thick
        forests outside Budapest,
the land subdivided when the wood
ran out. A language where people say
their last names first. An expert now,

I am invited to speak
at a gathering of poets and artists
on the subject of Hungarian art. I begin
with the violins, recite my mother's stories, her grandfather
courting with a gypsy band. I conjure Bartók, the tense and soaring
String Quartets, the darkening and apprehensive Sixth.
And the dark streets, the crowded Communist apartments and a
        foreboding
of the tanks, and before that, Theresienstadt.

These books are thick and large
and printed on heavy, shiny stock. The others
help me turn the pages, one by one, and together
we discuss the meaning of each work,

knowing nothing of the artists.
The bookshop a narrow spine between houses,
medieval, hidden, full of treasure, filled with cerebral pleasures
and small-scale aesthetics. My Hungarian family

was elegant. Old photographs show them
in aristocratic dress, the women's hair piled in elegant buns,
the men wearing waistcoats and watch fobs,
in drawing rooms of polished wood, crushed velvet and cut crystal. The
        women
wore hand-made underwear and served coffee and sacher torte
on tablecloths of delicate embroideries and lace. Who are these people
to whom I explain everything? Artists and poets, but they believe
I know what I'm talking about. Actually, I do,
though I haven't learned it in the usual way.
The man who invited me to speak puts his arm
around my shoulder, leads me into
the crowd. He looks like Will Inman. When I wake up
I'm still in the dream, can't open
my eyes. So I lie on the bed and try to join
the morning outside the window.
The dogs are barking at nothing,
the chickens make noise in response to the rooster,
and down the hall my family makes breakfast,
watches the news. I want an explanation
or a chance to rewind the film. I want to get up and put on
a Bartok record, but I don't, I wait until I realize

there's really nothing to explain. Then later that day
a catalog arrives. A bargain book—*Hungarian Art: the Twentieth
        Century Avant-Garde.*
All here, except the violin. A painting of a carousel
could be a violin. Forests, trees in a City Park,
trees behind and beneath
a seated woman's knees.
a 1937 untitled painting by Lajos Vajda (Vajda Lajos is how he would
        have signed it)

three houses in his village, the inside of a room, a manuscript
in English, German, Magyar, and in Hebrew script and print...
I cannot read them all...

Then Vajda's colleague Amos Imre, drawing dark houses and horses and
an angel/woman in the midst of war,
murdered in Germany,
nineteen forty four, and
sixteen years later his wife Anna Margit
paints a shouting woman
with the tethered feet
of a bird.

TRANSYLVANIA

Zoltan Frank, Kolosvár, 1919

My ancestors in Transylvania
must have shivered during thunderstorms
when the lightning lit the towers of the Count's castle
and seemed to float above the treetops

and when they moved from their forest hamlets
first to the yellow-stuccoed town of Újhely
and then to the big city, Kolosvár
they might have thought that they'd escaped
from the terror of forest darkness

but the roofs of Kolosvár
echoed, in their rows and rows of slate-gray peaks,
the shapes of nature, granite crags and pine trees,
and here it was not the Count
but the Prince himself
who could control a doctor's life
threaten him

so he would change his religion
change his name
and flee to Mexico,
taking his fine cigars.

Olga, Zoltan, and Erzsika Frank, Kolosvár, no date

THE MORTGAGE

Enny Friedman Hollós, Cegléd, 1929-1930

They say you marry someone like your father, but my father wasn't like that when I knew him.

Of course, I barely knew my father, growing up. I have a few memories of him, picking me up and laughing and kissing me, and I remember watching him sitting at my mother's bedside, holding her hand and speaking so quietly I could not hear what he was saying. After that, I lived with Aunt Margit and Uncle Arnold and remember my father coming once a year to visit, and bringing my brother Miksa. They would come from America and bring me funny little toys and poorly-made dresses that fell apart the first time Aunt Margit's maid Aggie washed them in the tub out in the courtyard.

I saw my other brother, Sandor, from time to time, but he didn't live with us when I was really young. Mostly he was away at school up in Hommona, living with some of Father's cousins. He came to Kolosvár for gimnázium, though, but he lived with Uncle Hubert, the Catholic surgeon. He always joined us for Sabbath dinner, though, and talked about the new economic theories he was studying, and about a Shakespeare play he'd actually read in English. Some days I'd see him walking through town, elegant and wordly. He went off to Vienna when I was only nine, though, and now he's in Canada.

Miksa was funny, he never went to one school long enough to learn anything. When he did come to Hungary, sometimes he'd live with us, sometimes with Uncle Hubert. He'd play with me more than Sandor ever did, but sometimes it was hard to understand him, he'd forgotten how to speak Hungarian, and he had no interest at all in the beautiful needlework I was learning to do or even in my piano playing.

Father made sure I had enough money to go to school, to take music lessons, but I really didn't think about him that much except when he visited. Mostly I spent time with my cousins, Olga and Erzsika, taking walks or talking about the concerts we'd gone to or the books we were reading, or about the young men we'd seen. When we had new dresses, we'd stop in at the photography studio on Matyás Király Tér and have our picture taken together, and send prints to our Grandmother Reichard back in Újhely and to Father and Miksa in America. Olga and Erzsika loved sending photo postcards of themselves to Miksa, they pretended he was their boyfriend and wrote charming messages on the card.

I first met Pál when I was invited to spend the summer in Budapest. I was 20, I'd been studying music with a distinguished teacher in Kolosvár, and she suggested that I go to the capital so that I could hear the finest musicians play, improve my own ear. Cousin Erno and his new bride invited me, and I was thrilled with the adventure that I would have. Pál had been a Lieutenant in the war, and when I first saw him, he was still wearing his uniform, tall and handsome in the blue suit with its gold trim. He and Erno had served together, and Pál had asked him to introduce me when I came.

I went back to Kolosvár in August, and Pál wrote to me every week. He was studying law now in Budapest, and he wrote about the elegance of philosophy and the practicalities of commerce. He suggested that I arrange once more to visit my cousin, and he need not have hinted so strongly, because I had already decided that perhaps I should move to Budapest. Olga, of course, had woven a delicious tale of our romance, and I loved to talk to her about Pál almost as much as I enjoyed his company when we were able to be together.

I wrote a long letter to Father and promised him that when he came to Hungary on his next trip, he would have the opportunity to meet Pál himself. "I know you will find much in common with him," I said. "He is a real patriot, and he enjoys music and a fine meal as you do."

The wedding was set for July, 1922. Father arrived in May and announced that he would buy a house for us. Pál had begun a legal practice in Cegléd, the small town southeast of Budapest where he had grown up. In June the transaction was completed and the home at 1

Ady Endre U. was ours—six rooms, a large covered porch on two sides, a charming courtyard with grapevines and peach trees. How fine to be the wife of a professional man, the mistress of my own home! And I was so pleased with Father, helping to make my dream come true. And of course, he brought photographs from America, of Miksa and his new wife and their little daughter Ruth, who they had named for our dear mother Rezi, "of blessed memory," I thought automatically, even if I really couldn't remember her. "I hope they will be able to visit you here," Father said as he toasted me and Pál and our new home, but I knew that they would not be likely to have the money to make such a trip. They had sent a silver platter as a wedding present, but it wasn't as nice as the ones we could have gotten in Budapest.

Then Father announced that he had sold his drugstore business and was retired, and now that I was married, he would divide his time equally among his three children. For the first time in my memory, my father would be living with me, at least for six months at a time! Pál wasn't so sure this was a good idea, but he knew how much it meant to me, and he agreed. And how could he object, since Father had paid for our home?

Pál was busy establishing his law practice. He spent almost every evening at the Club, making important contacts to develop business. Of course he knew most of the members from school and from his service in the Army. Cegléd was a small town, but there was work to be done, transfers of farm property, contracts for the sale of wheat and livestock, construction contracts for the new houses in town and for the industrial buildings going up on the outskirts, freight arrangements, and the occasional estate administration. Pál complained that the work wasn't as elegant as the theories he'd studied at University, but his clients were interesting men to spend time with, and the opportunity to draft an elegant document presented adequate intellectual stimulation.

Still, I wished we could spend more evenings together, sitting on our porch drinking coffee, talking about music or planning a trip to the spa at Héviz or even to an art exhibit in Budapest.

Olga had gotten married, too, and she and Mihaly had settled in Budapest. After the war Kolosvár had been cut off from Hungary, was now part of Romania, and as many Hungarians as could had moved into the center that remained of our once great nation. Erzsika was back in Újhely, so we didn't see her as much.

"Come for a few days," Olga said in her letter. "The train ride is not difficult, not much more than an hour each way, and you will have time to enjoy the children if you come alone." To my surprise, when I told Pál I was going to visit my cousin, he agreed, but added that he would meet me at the end of the week and we could spend the entire weekend at the Grand Hotel.

It was wonderful, like a second honeymoon with Pál. He acted as though he had no cares, he enjoyed the elegance of the hotel dining room with me, and we strolled arm in arm to the Opera House and allowed ourselves to be enveloped by the joy of Mozart's *Magic Flute*.

Our son Bondi was born late in January. He was the answer to my prayers, and he filled his father's dreams. "He will be a fine Hungarian officer," Pál said, looking down at the sweet face in the cradle. But while he loved Bondi, Pál spent little time at home. "It's too noisy," he'd say after dinner. "I'm going to the club where I can read quietly, and do some business."

Cegléd, November 1929

My dearest Father,

I hope that this letter finds you well, and that you receive it before you leave Pittsburgh for Montreal. You must be enjoying spending time with your darling Ruthie and with the young boys. I only wish that we could visit with them! The photograph of Ruthie in her lace dress, with flowers in her hair, reminded me so of the photographs Olga and Erzi and I used to have made in Kolosvár to send to you and Miksa and to our beloved Grandmama Reichard.

Bondi is doing well, he has grown so much since your visit last year, and when you return you will hardly recognize him! I am sending you a photograph of him playing with the little horses you gave him. Some day he could be a fine cavalry officer like his father.

Pál and I are well, but Pál's office has suffered some difficulties because of the great fall in the prices the estate owners received for their wheat and barley this year. He is so worried, Father. I try to help him look to the future, but I am afraid he thinks I am just a woman who doesn't understand such things. Almost every night he goes to the club, he says he can arrange a loan with one of the bankers he plays cards with there.

Father, I do hate to ask you once again for your help, you have been more than generous with us. But if you could help now, we will certainly secure the loan with another mortgage on the house. I know that you will not be here until next fall to make the arrangements at City Hall, but perhaps you could advance us 500 forints until then. I am unsure how much that will be for you in American dollars, and I know that there are problems now with the exchanges. But if there is anything that you can do, please write to me with your thoughts.

My love to Miksa and Emalene and the dear children.

Your beloved daughter,

Enny

Montreal, December 1929

My dear Enny,

I did receive your letter while I was still in Pittsburgh, although I was packing to leave for Sandor's that week. I apologize for not replying sooner, but I have just now gotten settled. I have made arrangements with the Bank of Canada to transfer funds to Sandor's old bank in Vienna, and they will send the funds on to you as soon as possible. I hope that this will help. Please make sure that you and Bondi have everything you may need before you give the rest to Pál for his office expenses. He must learn to get his affairs in order, although I appreciate how difficult the times are. This is becoming a world-wide depression, and I am afraid that the hard times of Hungarian farmers are not unique. I am thankful that you have your lovely home and especially that you and Pál have each other. When I see you together, it reminds me of what might have been between me and your dear mother, of blessed memory. She was so beautiful. Dear Enny, I wish you would have known her.

If you need to communicate with Herr Grumann in Vienna, who you met when I was in Budapest last year, remember that to him Sandor's name is Alex. He should be able to take care of all of the arrangements, though.

I will be traveling on the Queen Beatriz in September, and I'll give you more details when I have them. I do hope that you and Pál and Bondi will all come to meet me at Le Havre. It will be an exciting excursion for your handsome son!

Your loving Father.

Cegléd, February 1930

Gerson Mihalyné
Budapest

My dearest Olga,

I had to write to my father for money again, and he is sending it, and he was more than kind and generous in his response to my request, but how can I continue to ask him? Tell me, my dearest cousin, sister, how do you and Mihaly manage so well? You have two children, I only have one, and I live in a small town and have so few of the expenses you do. And we have our lovely garden, full of grapes and peaches and cabbages and all the delicacies you must buy at the market!

I would love to visit you, but Bondi is starting school and I am so busy. Can you and your entire family come to Cegléd soon? Perhaps you could come for a week-end. Oh, I long for our long walks through the public gardens of Kolosvár!

With fondest kisses,

Enny

Budapest, February 1930

Dear Enny,

We would love to come to visit. I wish you had a phone! We just got one, and if you go to the post office you can call us. The number is 2-345. Just ask the operator for Budapest, for that number. Then we can discuss all the details.

Oh, I want to talk to you too the way we used to. You know, they say you marry a man like your father. You don't realize it, but Pál is so much like your father was before your dear mother died. My mother used to tell me stories! She never wanted you to know, though. I think she promised your mother, when she was dying, that she'd take care of you and bring you up because they both knew your father couldn't do that, especially if he insisted on going back to America. But she told me things. I think because she wanted to make sure I didn't marry such a man.

Maybe that's why your father is so generous to you and Pál. He sees himself in Pál, the card games, the overreaching bets, the mistakes. He did all right, later, though, and now he can give it back to you. Maybe he thinks that he's making up for taking your mother away, who knows? Don't be afraid to ask. You'll never be able to change Pál.

Please, go to the post office and call me. You can find the money for the call, it really isn't that much. I can't wait to see you. We'll go for some long walks.

Your loving cousin,

Olga

Enny, Bondi, Cegléd, 1925

William Friedman Hungarian Residence Permit, 1936

Bondi, Enny, Pál, Aunt Bella, Cegléd 1936

PAPRIKA

My grandfather longed for Hungarian *gulyás*—
a soup he could barely remember,
the taste of paprika unlike anything
in America. His Galizianer wife
wasn't about to even try
to make it for him. They fought about it—
she'd sneer, recalling something greasy
he'd once gotten her to taste
in the Hungarian restaurant on Second Avenue.

The spice he searched for in his life
hangs in strings across the grocer's window
on Castle Hill in Budapest, looking
like chile ristras here at home.
I can't wait to taste the real thing
and I do—*gulyás* soup, paprika fish
with and without sour cream.
My mother sneers—the fish is full of bones
but I'm warmed by the rich red sauce
as hot as chile, and sometimes
by slices of crisp green pepper
with a bite and a lingering fire
stronger than any jalapeno.

Oh, my heritage is in these plants
that traveled from Mexico to Spain
and then to Hungary,
that travel back to Arizona now,
seeds tucked into an empty film can.

I'll cook the soup that Grandpa dreamed of,
grow this spice in Grandpa's memory.

Paprika hanging in store window and at door, Budapest, 1997

Paprikás ponty, Sátoraljaújhely, 2004

Paprika at Balatonfüred market, 2004

TWO SETS OF COURT DOCUMENTS, SHOWING STATUS OF ENNY FRIEDMAN HOLLÓS' REAL PROPERTY IN CEGLÉD AND BUDAPEST FOLLOWING THE HOLOCAUST

ORPHANS' COURT OF THE CITY OF CEGLÉD
1718/1945

Re: The guardianship/trusteeship of Dr. Hollós Pálné, whose address in unknown

Final Decision:
The orphans' court places Dr. Hollós Pálné [born Anna Friedmann] in the charge of a guardian...to be her husband, Dr. Hollós Pál, resident of Cegléd...   The orphans' court placed Dr. Hollós Pálné under guardianship/trusteeship....because in June of the last year she was deported to an unknown location; since then no word has been heard from her to suggest she is still alive, and because no trustee or guardian has been designated to handle her estate in her absence or in the event of her death.   The orphans' court has since appointed her husband as trustee/guardian, as is fitting in the eyes of the law, especially since no legal objection is known to the court.

September 25, 1945.
Dr. József Orosz
Administrator of the Orphans' Court

RESPECTED ORPHANS' COURT:

I, the undersigned, Dr. Hollós Pál, who, in her absence, was ordered to be the trustee of Dr. Hollós Pálné [Anna Friedman], hereby declare that she has arrived home from her deportation. Consequently, the reason for her having been placed in trusteeship no longer exists.

Sincerely,

Dr. Hollós Pál, Esq.

ORPHANS' COURT OF CEGLÉD
2627/1945

Subject: Removal of Dr. Hollós Pálné's estate from trusteeship

Final Decision:
The orphans' court has set aside its final decision no. 1718/1945 and seeks to stop the transfer of Dr. Hollós Pálné's personal estate into trusteeship.

Explanation:
Dr. Hollós Pál has announced that his wife has returned following her deportation. The orphans' court acknowledges his announcement and has reversed/stopped the transfer of Dr. Hollós Pálné's estate into trusteeship.

Drafted by the orphans' court of Cegléd on December 1st, 1945.

Signed & stamped
József Orosz
Administrator of the Orphans' Court

(provided by the International Red Cross; translated by Patrick Hartnett & Katalin Ori)

THE LAWYER

Hollós Pál, Budapest, October 1945

I've been a lawyer for more than twenty years. There have been good years and not-so-good years, but there have always been my clients, for whom I've prepared contracts and agreements, negotiated transactions to buy and sell homes, offices, and crops, and I've helped many of my clients with guardianships for elderly parents or orphaned children, and I've written their wills and administered their estates.

But since the War there have been few clients. So many of my Jewish friends are gone. No one has any money. Gyula covered for me after the Jewish laws took effect, took possession of everything I could transfer to him. He used this office, which was his property to start with. He maintained my furnishings and paid my secretary.

But now I'm back from the front, somehow still alive. I come to the office every day, because what else is there for me to do? Bondi was killed before the War. And Enny is gone. I have no idea if she is still alive or if she was one of the murdered ones. I do not know where was taken. I have heard nothing from anyone who might have seen her in any of the camps.

Trains arrive in Budapest every day and survivors and refugees straggle through the city, trying to locate any other surviving family and friends, trying to find some food to eat and a place to stay, trying to find a way to get home to their old towns and villages, or deciding they have a better chance if they stay here.

So what could I do...to keep her properties, now that the Jewish laws are over—the house in Cegléd and the pied-a-terre here in Budapest—I had to file guardianship papers, and the court in Cegléd appointed me Enny's guardian and trustee of her property and notified the court in Budapest. How strange, to write out the very documents I have written so many times, but this time with Enny's name, and mine as her guardian, and the reason "because in June of the last year she was deported to an unknown location; since then no word has been heard from her to suggest she is still alive." I wrote these words as though I were her lawyer, but of course I am her husband, I love her, and I have dreams and nightmares, because there has been no word to suggest she is still alive, and yet every day I see someone who is still alive. But I wrote the words and dressed in a suit and stood before the Court.

Budapest, December 1945

Enny has returned home! She is weak, although for six months she has been cared for by the Americans. Thank God, she has returned home!

I came back to my office and drafted declarations to each court that she is home, and alive, and that the guardianship should be terminated. Writing these words felt so little like being a lawyer. The words are dry on the page, like any words a lawyer writes, but I wrote them with a strong and joyous heart, a husband's heart.

Page 1.) of 5 [on the original document]:

Orphans' Court of the City of Cegléd

1718/1945.sz.   Re: The guardianship / trusteeship of Dr. Hollós Pálné, whose
                                 address is unknown

FINAL DECISION.

The orphans' court places Dr. Hollós Pálné [born Anna Friedmann] in the charge of a guardian, on the
basis of point d.) of the law of 1877: XX. t.c. paragraph 28. The guardian is to be her husband, Dr. Hollós
Pál, resident of Cegléd, whom the court orders to represent her personal, financial, and property 'estate'
with fatherly dedication and responsibility, as is demanded of him in the attached guardianship law.

The orphans' court turns to the central district court of Budapest, as registrar of property deeds, and
requests the court note that Dr. Hollós Pálné [Anna Friedmann], partial owner of the real estate situated
on the left bank of the Danube at Budapest [house number 32935 on the and row of land certificate
number 971], has been placed under guardianship by this court because of her absence.

The orphans' court requests the guardian, Dr. Hollós Pál, make a recommendation within 30 days as to
the handling of the estate in question.

Finally, the orphans' court orders that an inventory of the estate under trusteeship be made within 15 days.

Explanation:

The orphans' court placed Dr. Hollós Pálné under guardianship / trusteeship on the basis of point d. of the
law of 1877: XX. t.c. (paragraph?) 28, because in June of the last year she was deported to an unknown
location; since then no word has been heard from her to suggest she is still alive, and because no trustee or
guardian had been designated to handle her estate in her absence or in the event of her death. The
orphans' court has since appointed her husband as trustee / guardian, as is fitting in the eyes of the law,
especially since no legal objection is known to the court.

An appeal may be made with regard to this decision within 15 days of the receipt of this letter. Any
appear must be delivered to the undersigned.

To be notified: public trustee; Dr. Hollós Pál, resident of Cegléd; with the extract of the orphans' law, and
the district court of Budapest, as the registrar of property deeds.

Signed (original signature)
Dr. József Orosz
Administrator of the orphans' court

Stamp of Certification
9069 / 2002.... I officially certify that this numbered document is an exact copy of the no. 1841 / 1946
document in the possession of the orphans' court of the city of Cegléd, which is managed by the archives
of the city of Pest.

Signed László Böőr Director of Archives
Nagykőrös, April 15th, 2002

Enny's house in Cegléd

Enny's apartment building, 20 Verseny U., Budapest

THE TABLECLOTH

(Enny's Dream, 1947)

I'm dreaming I'm part of the procession. The wedding procession that marches around the sides of the tablecloth—the gold-and-silver brocade cloth Father gave me—was it for our tenth wedding anniversary? Yes, in 1932. He had just returned from Montreal. Later, after I'd had it for awhile, I think when I was telling him how much I'd enjoyed using it at the dinner party I gave for Pál's partner and his wife, Father told me that he'd bought three of these cloths, at that wonderful linens shop near Andrassy Avenue. The one, of course, he'd given to me. And he'd given one to Sandor's wife Sadie and one to Miksa's daughter Ruthie, for her trousseau, even though she didn't even have a boyfriend then. (But now she's gotten married, Miksa sent me a photograph from the wedding, that red-headed girl standing under a chuppah of flowers and leaves right there in the same living room where her mother and I had our big quarrel—if you can call it a big quarrel when we didn't even speak the same language! Anyway, I hope Ruthie uses that tablecloth in good health.)

This tablecloth depicts an Eastern Orthodox wedding—one procession on each side of the long cloth—the priest with his mitre and scepter, the bride wearing a headress of flowers, the groom elegant in an embroidered vest. And the rest of the procession follows—the ringbearers, cupbearers, nosegay-bearers—all attired so elegantly, all dignified but clearly pleased as they march to the strains of violins and flutes coming from the back of the line.

When was the last time I'd used that cloth? I didn't use it often, it really was only appropriate for wedding parties and anniversaries. It was when Olga and Mihaly visited us, a few months before we were taken

71

away. It wasn't an anniversary, really—their anniversary had been a month earlier, and they'd wanted us to spend the week with them at the lake to celebrate, but with the new laws we weren't able to take a villa there. So when they came to Cegléd in March we had a sort of belated anniversary dinner. I served paprika chicken, Olga's favorite, of course, and the first radishes from the garden, and after dinner we had a bottle of Tokaj Aszú with dobostorte and then brandy. But Bondi was not with us, he'd gone off to Budapest, "to try to do something about things," meaning the anti-Jewish actions and the Nyilas—the Arrow Cross, the fascists, he said.

In the dream, I am in the procession. Not the bride, but one of the attendants. I'm carrying flowers, roses, and my skirt falls softly to my ankles, and my shoes buckle across the top of my feet, and my hair and my skin and my dress and my shoes and the roses are all a subtle tone of silver, and the world around me is a soft dusty gold. And Pál is there as well, another attendant, his silver hair rendered accurately by the silver threads, and we are marching to the wedding, and Bondi follows, a little ring-bearer.

But of course we are not marching to any wedding, we are marching through a narrow stone gate into Terezin Fortress in Czechoslovakia and there is no wedding and there is no banquet and there are no roses and there is no Bondi, and there are no rings, and nothing is gold and nothing is silver and Pál and I are not marching together and I will not see him for eight months but Rosza sees glimpses of him when she delivers the piles of folded laundry and she reports to me that he looks well, he is tall and so she always sees his face and his silver hair above the heads of the rest of the men's battalion as they march out to wherever they are put to work, and she always recognizes Pál and she always reports to me and that is how I survived there, that and the stories we women told each night, lying in our bunks, the recipes...

But in the dream now we are being pulled—the whole line of us, marching, pulled, and the whole world of the golden cloth is being pulled—pulled—flipped up into the air, then folded, folded neatly, as we always fold such a tablecloth before putting it away in the cupboard, folded carefully, smoothing the folds, squaring the corners....

And in the dream the cloth is being picked up by a tall man, he looks like Pál but he's not—he's a soldier, in uniform—he's an American!—I can see the letters "US" on his uniform— and Pál and I have fallen out of the procession, out of the cloth, and I am lying on the floor and the American lifts up the cloth and unfolds enough to examine the design, recognizes the scene as a wedding procession, and I can understand enough of his English from the year I spent with Miksa and with Sandor in America, he is saying, "Good, I can give this to my daughter for her wedding," and there lying on the floor I am trying to shout, "No, No, my father gave me that cloth for my wedding anniversary, No, No..." but he folds it up again and walks with it through a wide polished wooden doorway into another room, and then I wake up.

"It can't be," Pál says. "The Americans liberated the camps. They wouldn't take our things. The Nazis, the Arrow Cross, yes, they took our things. Not the Americans. The Americans aren't even in Hungary. You are mistaken, my love." He brushes my hair away from my sweaty face with his long fingers. "You are mistaken, Enny. It's all right. Go back to sleep."

(excerpt from report of Presidential Advisory Commission on Holocaust Assets in the United States on the "Hungarian Gold Train," October 14, 1999)

> U.S. military personnel recognized from the beginning that the art and cultural property assets of the Gold Train were valuable and impressive and could be used in their offices and homes. On July 13, 1945, Major General Harry J. Collins, Commander of the 42nd ("Rainbow") Division in western Austria, received objects of "furniture and furnishing...supplied by Office of Property Control, Land Salzburg."
>
> General Collins also requisitioned valuables from the Gold Train for his home. An August 28, 1945 memo

from one of Collins' aides to the Property Control Officer in Salzburg made the following demand:

...

d) Thirty (30) sets of table linens, each set to consist of one table cloth and 12 napkins.)
...

Nor was General Collins the only military official who used the Gold Train property for personal use...General Laude received china, silverware and linen for his Salzburg home; General Hume received 18 rugs, table and silverware, table linen and glassware...

Source: "Progress Report On: The Mystery of the Hungarian 'Gold Train'", draft October 7, 1999, for release October 14, 1999, 5:00 pm, http://www.pcha.gov/goldtrainfinaltoconverthtml#AppropriationsoftheGoldTrainTreasures. Available from http://www.pcha.gov/991014gtbriefing.html, Briefing by Art Research Staff to the Presidential Advisory Commission on Holocaust Assets in the United States on the "Hungarian Gold Train," October 14, 1999.

Reported on NPR, October 14, 1999.

Héviz, 2004

Friedman family reunion, Héviz, 1936. At left: Bondi, Enny, William, Pál

AT HÉVIZ

Enny Friedman Hollós, Héviz, 1949

"Look, the Foto-Park still has a stand here at Héviz!" Olga's voice sounded genuinely surprised. "We should have our picture taken, just like we used to."

"I don't know," I said. "I mean...."

"Oh, please," Olga said. "And then we can send one to Sandor, and one to Miksa." She stopped, there on the path through the woods beyond the hotel, and turned to face me directly. "So they'll know we're all right." Then she started to walk again, slowly. "Let's get Pál and Mihaly, get our pictures taken to send to them."

"It's the first time we've been back to Héviz," I said. I wanted to just see if we could spend the week here, if we could enjoy ourselves. I was certainly enjoying walking along the curving paths, passing others strolling through the woods. It was a beautiful fall day. Just cool enough to be wearing our coats again. The trees still held onto their leaves, still dark green, and Olga was still wearing her open-toe white shoes. We walked slowly, slower than we had before.

"Have you written to them?" Olga asked me. This time I was the one to stop, and I turned to her.

"I tried to write to both of them when we first returned home," I said. "I couldn't find a way to say it then. But finally I did write, and I told them what I could. I told them Bondi was shot and Pál and I were in Thieresenstadt, that it was a work camp, but that we were home now."

"Did you tell them about Erzsi?"

"Only that we haven't heard from her. I told them you were fine."

"You could have stayed there, in America, in Canada..."

"Stop it. Let's get Pál and Mihaly and get these pictures taken." We started to walk again, turning off on a path that wound back to the hotel. A sparrow flew off as we passed a spent flower-bed where it was picking at fallen seed. I did always love coming to Héviz. So relaxing, the mineral baths, the views of Lake Balaton, the benches along the lake where you can sit and watch the small waves gentling lapping the shore, the coffee house, the lovely rooms with carved oak headboards and satin coverlets on the beds. I remembered the last time we were here, well before the war, in 1936. Father's last trip here before he died. It was a huge family reunion, all the Reichards and Friedmans. We were celebrating Father's 72nd birthday, and we all came, more than twenty of us, and we had our picture taken at the entrance to the resort. We sent that postcard to everybody, and I kept one under the glass on the table in the sitting room. I wish I still had that card, but when we came back from the camp, it was gone. Along with the other one I loved so, of Bondi playing on that little white bearskin rug. Bondi and Father, both gone.

As we came up to the hotel, Pál and Mihaly were there on the veranda, smoking. "Olga would like us to have our photograph taken again," I said. I'd begun to think it was a good idea. "So we could send the picture to Sandor and Miksa in America." Neither of our husbands had ever met my brothers, but a smile came over Pál's face immediately. "Of course," he said. "Olga is right. We should send them photographs of us on holiday. They probably do not believe we can go on holiday. Let's make the arrangements." He stood up and walked toward us. Pál still stood tall and straight, and as I watched him walk toward me, I felt like a young bride seeing her handsome husband for the first time. How could I have left him, stayed in America? He took my arm and helped me up the step to the chairs.

We had come to Héviz with our old friend Anna, the widow of Pál's friend, Sigmund Eisnitz, and Pál's partner Gyula Szentpetery and his wife. Gyula wasn't Jewish, and he'd managed to keep his wife hidden away somewhere after the Arrow Cross had come to Cegléd. "The Szentpeterys' should be in the photograph too, don't you think?" he said as we sat down. "Yes, of course," Olga said. "Why don't we ask them?" Of course, I had to think, they would share the cost of the photographer. But perhaps it wasn't important. I think Pál had transferred some of the assets of his practice to Jules, too, when things got bad, although I was never sure. It wasn't something Pál would have discussed with me.

Some gypsy musicians were coming out onto the veranda, getting ready to play during the afternoon tea. Waiters were beginning to set up tables with white lace cloths, silver tea service, platters of strudel and almond cookies.

"Let's sit here for awhile, have something to eat and listen to the music," I suggested. The gypsy music would remind me of Father. He used to hire a band to go with him when he went courting. I remember how strange my friends thought it was, this strange man visiting us, going out courting young women with his band. I always had to explain how my mother was dead, how Margit and Arnold weren't my parents, they were my aunt and uncle, how my father was just visiting from America. But I loved to listen to the gypsy melodies, to sing in my heart along with the violin, and to hope that the young woman might love Father enough to keep him here with us in Hungary. None of them ever did, but he did hire one of his favorite bands to play when Pál and I were married.

When the band did begin to play, we sat at our table, sipping our tea and nibbling at cherry strudel almost as fine as we used to have at Héviz. "Even the Communists can't take away our ability to enjoy cherry strudel!" Olga whispered as she handed me a plate.

"Let's get this photograph taken care of," Pál said, getting up from the table. "There's still enough light. I'll go and find the others." I watched his tall, straight back as he walked through the wide hotel door. I'll always be glad I married Pál, I thought. Despite everything.

After we'd gotten back home, I wrote to each of my brothers for only the second time since the end of the war. I folded the thin paper, and before I slipped one of the Héviz Foto-Park pictures into each envelope, I wrote the date on the back of the photos—October 9, 1949. It was ten years since I had seen either of my brothers, and so much had happened. Maybe I shouldn't do this, I thought, but then I sealed the envelopes, walked down to the Post Office, where the old red royal horns still designated the door, and I sent the photos off to America.

Héviz October 9, 1949: Back row: Hollós Pál, Gerson Mihaly, Szentpetery Gyula, Szentpetery Gyulané; front row: Hollós Pálné (Enny Friedman), Gerson Mihalyné (Olga Frank), Eisnitz Sigmundné (Anna)

Retés (strudel), Héviz,2004

80

I AM TRYING TO UNDERSTAND

Lynn, Cegléd, July 1997

I am trying to understand a woman
who chose handmade lingerie
over America
who returned to her husband
to a place where their son
would be shot

Whose hand sewed the yellow star
onto her coat?

I am trying to understand how, four years after
they returned from the camp
a man and a woman are smiling at the lake
they are there with her cousin and their friends
Seven people
enjoying their vacation

What have the healing waters at Héviz
been able to wash away?

I am trying to understand
what a woman who has lost her son can think
when she plants four-o-clocks and daisies
in her garden
where they once sat, reading

I am trying to understand how a woman like that
can plant any garden at all
how she could tend her grapevines

The Communists allowed them one room in their house

that had been a wedding present from her father
the house confiscated in 1944
"Jewish owner: title cleared"
Which room did they receive?
Had anyone kept
the lace cloths, the crocheted bedspread?
I am trying to understand—
Did she want them back?

I am trying to understand
how they told her that her son was dead
Did it happen at his school?
Were they taken to the camps the same day,
or the next?

I am trying to understand
why I am standing in Annie's courtyard
Why I bend down to smell the tarragon
and chervil growing among rocks
Why I photograph bunches of fat grapes
Why I think this could be mine

Enny's Grapes, Cegléd, 1997

Endre (Bondi) Hollós, probably 1938, Budapest

ROWS OF SYCAMORES, BALATONFÜRED

Lynn, Balatonfüred, 2004/Enny, 1928

> I touch God in my song
>> as the hill touches the far-away sea
>> with its waterfall.

> —Rabindranath Tagore, "Fireflies"

Rows of sycamores line Tagore Sétány,
the promenade along the lake
named for the Hindu poet
who came here for the cardiac cure.
I walk up and down the graceful path,
shaded by the trees that shaded Enny and Bondi
in 1928. I sit on a bench
and Michiko photographs me
in approximately the pose
Enny took, showing off her 3-year-old son.
The sycamores stand in parade formation
but green canopies can only be alive, relaxed.

Hungary, India, United States, Japan
linger under these trees. Landlocked
Balaton touches only Hungarian soil,
but we are all here, bringing
Atlantic and Pacific, Bay of Bengal,
Sea of Japan, Sea of Cortez,
even Kegon Falls.
I have come thousands of miles
to photograph this place, to sit
on a Victorian bench
as Enny did. It's been 76 years. Bondi

resisted the Nazis and found his grave
in the Duna. Enny lived to old age
and died under onion-dome turrets
at the Ujpest Home of Love.

Now I come here to sit
beneath these sycamores. How long
can a sycamore tree live?

Enny and Bondi, Balatonfüred, 1928

Lynn, Balatonfüred, 2004. Photo by Michiko Kameda.

DREAD, PEACE, after Radnoti

Lynn, Enny's House, VII Budapest, Verseny u. 20, 2004

> *halott néném jutott e szembe s már repült*
> *feletten mind, akit szerettem és nem él,*
> *sötéten szállt seregnyi néma holt,*
> *s egy árnyék dõlt el hirtelen a házfalon.*
> *Csend lett, a délelõtt megállt.*
>
> I thought of my dead aunt and in a flash it seems
> all the unliving I had loved were flying overhead,
> with hosts of silent dead the sky as darkened then
> and suddenly across the wall a shadow fell.
> Silence. The morning world stood still.
>
> —Radnóti Miklos
> *"Béke, Boryalom"* ("Peace, Dread"), 1938

I think of my dead aunt and in a flash it seems
all the unliving I had never known, but love,
are flying overhead
with hosts of silent dead the sky brightens
and suddenly across the wall a shadow falls. Silence.
The morning world stands still.

With a train ticket from Buchenwald, she came back to this house,
"laced under guardianship," the year I was born.
I knew she existed, my grandfather's sister who wrote him letters
from an ashen world. I had no way to meet her.
I knew she had a son the Nazis murdered. I knew
about murder, followed the Rosenberg case
on our new TV.
                    That's why I couldn't know her—
the Communists. My grandfather couldn't mail his sister

a package of stockings, a dress, some cash,
a photograph of me. He routed them through Canada,
through family there, their government less paranoid.
Impossible to visit.

Csókolom, I kiss your hand. Aunt Enny, I would have kissed your hand
if I'd been able. Instead, more than fifty years after
you sold this house, I track it down, find it
so close to Keleti Station, take photographs,
try to explain to the people who live there now.

I photograph the house, the courtyard, the garden. Your shadow
silent against the wall.
And the hosts of all the silent dead
whose names and numbers I have studied
brighten the sky. *Csókolom*, they whisper.
My morning world stands still.

LEARNING TO SAY
"SÁTORALJAÚJHELY"

Lynn, Sátoraljaújhely, 2004

My grandfather was a quiet man who visited us every Sunday and sat in a corner of our living room smoking a stogie and watching golf or football on TV. He seemed to have abandoned speech beneath the din of my grandmother's aggressive, opinionated gossip. But one Sunday when I was home from college, my father rigged up his new reel-to-reel tape recorder underneath our dining room table and specifically invited his father-in-law to tell us the story of his life.

"I was born in Oo-ee-hey," my grandfather started, spinning magical tales of his childhood in Hungary, his family's immigration to Brooklyn and subsequent return to Hungary, where he celebrated his Bar Mitzvah at his dying mother's bedside, and his adolescent adventures traveling back and forth between Hungary and Duquesne, a small town outside Pittsburgh. The stories that poured onto the tape were nothing like the stories I'd read about Eastern European immigrants living in tenements on the Lower East Side. Nor did they resemble the family legends from my Litvak and Galizianer aunts, whose families had come to America and were happy never to see their homes again.

I didn't think much about Grandpa's tape until I started seriously writing poetry in the early 1980s. Periodically I tried to track down the location of "Oo-ee-hey" on a map, without success. Admittedly, my grandfather's speech consisted mostly of mumbling in an accent that betrayed his lack of formal education. Besides "Oo-ee-hey," he'd mentioned "Oomvar" and some other sounds that didn't match anything on any map I could find. But most American Jews say their ancestors came from shtetls that "aren't on the map anymore." Then I started to haunt the University library, poring over the glowing green display screens of the newly-installed computerized catalog. I found

90

and started reading books about Hungary, about central European mythology, about different patterns of immigration to America. One day I came across a fascinating book, *Bridging Three Worlds*. There, in Robert Perlman's recital of his own journey to identify his family's roots, was that mysterious pronunciation:

> The sounds of the places, spoken in the soft, lilting Hungarian of my grandparents, have remained in my ears: *Sharoshpottock...Mishcolts...Ooey-hey*. It was many years before I saw those towns on a map as Sárospatak, Miskolc, and Újhely, whose full name is Sátoraljaújhely.

Perlman had decoded the mysterious syllables for me into a word that would be located in an index to a map: *Sátoraljaújhely*. I couldn't imagine how one was the same as the other.

In 1997 my mother sold the jewelry my grandfather had bought for my grandmother on their vacations in Atlantic City and Miami Beach so she could take my sister and me on a week's group tour to Hungary. We were only going to be in Sátoraljaújhely for a day, but my mother had located her father's birth record, and that of his brother, which identified the address where they were living when each was born as Kazinczy Utca 515, and also identified the *sandak*—the godfather, who holds the baby during circumcision—for each of them: someone named Reichard David—wine trader. Our smaller group of six who had roots in Sátoraljaújhely spent most of the day poring over original archival record books from 1857 through 1891, and located not only the original records of my grandfather's and great-uncle's births, but the marriage record of their parents, my great-grandparents, and the record of a third child born to them, a baby boy who died at ten days of age, too ill for a *bris*, unnamed. A notation on the record said "the father has emigrated to America." My mother, sister and I gasped simultaneously: we'd all heard the story that William Friedman had been kicked out of Europe for his gambling debts. This record seemed to prove that—he'd left his pregnant wife and two boys in Újhely, rushing off to Brooklyn to make a livelihood he'd lost in the casinos that, for some reason, attracted many middle-class Hungarian Jewish men at the end of the 19th century.

After leaving the archives, we started to walk down Kazinczy Utca, which starts just to the east of the square where the archives are located. Beautiful art nouveau style townhouses and charming hanging flower bowls grace the street, but we walked further and further without getting anywhere near "515." We asked directions from a young boy who was studying English in school and was happy to practice it; he advised us that the 515 address would be too far to walk, we should take the bus. Meanwhile our driver returned with others from our group who had gone to their ancestral village for a few hours, and we asked him to drive us down the road. He denied that such a large house number even exists in Hungary, but proceeded down the road. Soon, however, we came to the Slovakian border. In 1920, the Trianon treaty that ended World War I divided Hungary, and the town of Újhely, giving half of Greater Hungary's territory to Czechoslovakia, Ukraine, and Romania. We turned around to return to our hotel in Nyíregyháza, but not far down the road we noticed a building that looked like a synagogue, and stopped. It turned out to be a cemetery, with the *chevra kadisha* building, and inside we found a dedication plaque: the cemetery was founded in 1886 by the Status Quo community—and there, on the list of donors, was the *sandak*, Reichard David.

I vowed to return to Újhely as soon as I could. Surely this cemetery held the remains of many in my family.

In the summer of 2004, I had an opportunity to return. I'd been working on poems and stories about my Hungarian family, exhibiting photographs and doing multi-media presentations, and I'd been awarded an artists' residency at Balatonfüred, a resort on Lake Balaton, the inland sea of Hungary, where my grandfather's sister and her family had vacationed. I'd be spending time in Budapest as well, and it seemed obvious that I should return to Sátoraljaújhely. But could I manage it alone? I couldn't even pronounce the name of the town, and I knew that no one there would speak English.

I started doing Internet searches, trying to find out whether there was a place to stay and what it would take to get there. I found a wonderful city-sponsored site, Sátoraljaújhely.hu, and although it was in Magyar, there were lots of pictures, and I was able to slowly figure out a lot of the text with the minimal knowledge I'd acquired and the help of a good bilingual dictionary. I found the train schedules and fares readily available online. It would take about a three hour train trip costing about $20 to get from centrally located Budapest to Sátoraljaújhely, at the far northeast tip of Hungary. At my favorite used book store in Tucson, I found a small Berlitz Hungarian phrasebook, with a clear pronunciation guide—there are no diphthongs, just pronounce each syllable—and just enough grammar to help me overcome my confusion at the varying prefixes, suffixes, and compound words that dominate the language, which is completely unrelated to any of the other languages I've learned. Then an email contact with a Reichard relative let me know about a hotel where the manager not only spoke English but could communicate by email. I made reservations for three nights at $40 a night. I was going back to Újhely!

On June 28, the afternoon after arriving in Budapest, still unable to communicate much in Magyar let alone clearly pronounce "Sátoraljaújhely," I managed to scribble my request to the ticket agent at Keleti Station in Budapest and hop on the Intercity train to Szerencs with only a minute to spare. In my compartment, a young boy of maybe 10 was traveling with his grandmother and another older woman, who didn't get off when the boy and his grandmother did at Miskolcs. He was carrying a fishing rod, and I was able to understand a little of the two women, discussing between themselves recipes for fish, including *gombas* (mushrooms) and *halászlé* (fish soup) and *paprika*. Watching the boy hug his grandmother, I smiled to myself and remembered how my grandfather used to take my youngest brother fishing—the only Jews I knew who liked to fish.

At Szerencs I switched to the local to Újhely, an older, grungier train filled with vacationing college students, noisy and laughing, carrying fishing poles and camping equipment. When we arrived at the

Sátoraljaújhely station, large groups of younger children were gathered in front, waiting, with adults, a summer-camp group. The hills and rivers around Újhely are now a major outdoor recreation area, a favorite not only of Hungarians but of students from Eastern Europe and the Middle East.

On the wall outside the railroad station I saw the memorial plaque that had just been installed a few weeks earlier, commemorating the 60th anniversary of the deportations to Auschwitz. The plaque has a relief of a train car with people desperately waving out the window, appropriately macabre. The installation of this plaque, funded by the Jewish and Jehovah's Witness communities, was the purpose for the Reichards' visit that had facilitated my own.

I wasn't able to find anyone at the station who could speak English or understand my almost-non-existent Magyar well enough to explain how best to get to my hotel, so I studied the large map board under the trees next to the station, started walking, asked *"hol van…"* several times, and found the Hotel Henriette. The manager, Ignacz Idilko, who had emailed me, was a charming young woman who spoke English and showed me to the huge room that would be my home during my four day visit to my grandfather's town.

After a brief rest, I took my camera and went out to revisit the places I'd been 7 years earlier. The city hall was closing up and cleaners were sweeping the lobby, where the photograph of Jewish businesses I'd seen in 1997 had been replaced with a large folding-board exhibit on Hungary's entrance into the European Union. I picked up a helpful little brochure which described the town's high points in Magyar, German, and English and included an excellent street map labeling every street in town and numbering the attractions. Then I walked past the little shop where we'd bought ice cream—it was hard to see the window signs because awnings reading "Stella Artois" had been installed and a little sidewalk café had been created, but I bought a "bounty" gelato cone, a mixture of coconut and chocolate, and I walked around the familiar streets, savoring the sweetness.

For dinner I returned to the Halász Csárda (fish restaurant) where we'd eaten in 1997, and managed to order (in Magyar) *ponty* (carp) Sátoraljaújhely-style (with a paprika-sour cream sauce) and a mixed salad and mineral water. I collected another little Hungarian flag like the one that I'd taken from our meal there in 1997 and paid about $5.00 for my delicious dinner.

The next morning, I woke up early, thinking about walking in the town where my grandfather was born, where his grandmother had supported her four little girls by peddling soda water she'd bottled herself from a donkey cart she drove up and down these hilly streets. Later, I went to the Múzeum, picked up a photocopied three-page English-language summary of the museum's contents, and studied the Magyar labels for the stuffed birds posed naturalistically among dead twigs and leaves, photographs of cows in a flat field below hills with a small castle, beautiful photographs of wildflowers.

Painstakingly, I wrote out the Magyar and Latin names and my descriptions in my journal: *Hálaszsas, Pandion haliaetus*—fish eagle; *sárgarigó, Oriolus oriolus*—golden oriole, *méregőlő sisakuirág, aeon itum anthora*—yellow. And an exhibit of rocks and geology—opals are mined here, and I remembered how my grandfather always loved opals, despite the American superstition that they're bad luck. Lots of rhyolites (*riolit*) and basalts (*basalt*) and other volcanic-looking rock in the exhibit made me feel at home, as these same rocks form the landscape of Tucson, and I copied into my journal two paragraphs of still-untranslated Magyar explanation of the volcanic activity in the region 11-12 million years ago.

The Múzeum also contains displays of the history of the area, explaining how the first *aszu* wine—the fine dessert wine now produced primarily in nearby Tokaj—was first made in Újhely in the 17th century by a priest named Lackó Máté. Beautiful grape-relief ceramics and glass are displayed. An exhibit explains that the town hall was built by the Empress Maria Theresa (1740-1780) and József II (1780-1790). But the major emphasis here is on Kazinczy Ferenc, the famous 18th century writer whose house this building once was. His furniture, including the desk he used while working in the room that is now the Town Hall Archives (where we searched for and found our ancestors' records in 1997) are displayed. There is a reconstruction of the casino that once operated in this building, where Kossuth Lajos, the architect of the short-lived 1848 revolution, spent his time with like-minded literary and political gentlemen. A large photograph of Kossuth hangs on the wall along with an engraving of the 1848 call to independence and a collection of revolutionary documents, along with the proclamation by the Emperor Ferencz József ending the revolution. An 1836 map displayed on the wall shows this casino, next to it the synagogue, and across the street, the home of a Jewish family.

The one English-speaking employee of the Múzeum, a young woman, came by to interpret for me and answer questions. She was helpful, but I felt I had to move quickly rather than linger meditatively among the evocative exhibits. And her priorities were different. I knew that my great-grandfather was a card player who left Sátoraljaújhely in a hurry because of his gambling debts. When I asked my guide whether there were other casinos in Sátoraljaújhely, she answered, "Yes, there were others, but they weren't important." Next time, I'll write out the words for "I'd like to take some more time here on my own." As it was, all I could say was "Köszönöm," thank you.

That afternoon, I walked up the tent-shaped hill for which the city is named, through beautiful forest, to the Magyar Kalvaria monument, built in 1936 to memorialize the Hungarian towns lost in the Trianon treaty. Black volcanic stone pillars are set along the winding dirt road to the top of the hill, using the concept of the Stations of the Cross, bearing ceramic and plaster relief plaques with the coats-of-arms of each lost town, bearing images of grapes, sheaves of wheat, fish, oak leaves, and sentimental poetic inscriptions to eternally reclaim these towns which by fiat became Czech, Slovak, Romanian, Italian, Ukrainian. As I walked, I wondered how this related to Hungarian Jews. I know that my families included people from these towns—some became cut off from their relatives in Hungary; others moved to Budapest or elsewhere. But did the Hungarian patriots who erected these monuments blame the Jews for this loss of sovereignty? By 1936

Hungarian anti-Semitism was growing, was noticeable enough that my grandfather and his brother brought their sister and her son to America, although they couldn't convince her to stay. At the top of the hill is a shrine topped with the national symbol, St. Stephen's Cross, containing an altar covered with handmade lace; on the other side of the hilltop, facing the city, is a stone terrace from which flies the Hungarian flag. A few couples walked onto the plaza while I was there; one greeted me with "*Jó napot*" and then an older couple actually tried to chat with me, but I had to reply "*nem beszél Magyar*—I don't speak Hungarian" and so they smiled and said "*bocsánot, viszontlátásra*," to which at least I could reply, "*viszontlátásra*, good bye." I felt sorry I couldn't converse more fully, but at least I didn't have to act stupid.

It rained a little as I strolled down the hill, stopping to photograph wildflowers. I went for a delightful vegetarian dinner to Kövesudvar Etterem, which had advertised its vegetarian offerings on the Sátoraljaújhely.hu website. The waiter there greeted me with "*Csókolom,*" I kiss your hand, the formal expression that made my grandfather want to return to informal America.

My primary objective in returning to Sátoraljaújhely had been to spend time in the cemetery we'd discovered at the end of our short visit in 1997. I'd written to the contact name and address I'd kept from that trip but hadn't received an answer. When I returned to my hotel after my day full of adventures, there was a message from Idilko saying that she'd reached the cemetery key-holder who would meet me at 10 in the morning.

The next morning, I walked the mile or so up Kazinczy Utca to the cemetery. When I got there, I found that the building had been significantly expanded and painted, and the caretaker, whose phone numbers were posted at the door, now lived in a house attached to the *chevra kadisha* building. He wound up showing me around the cemetery, having asked me what my family names were. (I hadn't written them down, and wished I had, as not all the relevant names came to mind quickly under his methodical pressure.) When I mentioned the name Czinner, he immediately asked, "Dr. Czinner?" and showed me at least one stone with that title in front of the name. (My grandfather's stories involved several doctors, all without last names. He had mentioned that his dying mother returned to Hungary from Brooklyn to be treated by an uncle who was a doctor—one of her mother's brothers, who would have been named "Czinner.") The caretaker knew where all the families were buried. Although he didn't speak English, he was able to answer my questions in basic Hungarian and ask me some basic questions as well, and we both used a lot of repetition and speaking slowly and pointing and gestures.

The cemetery was still overgrown with blackberry brambles and weeds, but there was a wide path plowed up the center, and the caretaker pushed the thorny canes and larger weeds aside with his cane. There were times when we had to step over fallen tombstones, which felt disturbing, but we managed to walk all over the cemetery. We focused on an area with many Czinners and Reichards. Unfortunately, since I was being led on a tour rather than left on my own, I didn't have time to do much more than make quick identification of names and take as many photographs as I could to study later. Many of the stones bore Hungarian names and dates (in the Roman alphabet), but I could also identify many by their Hebrew names. A large stone next to that of David Reichard (the wine trader and *sandak*) bore the Hebrew name *Hani*, my great-great grandmother's name, but there was another woman, buried on the other side of David, who was identified as his wife, whose death date was after the time when we believe he would have been married to Hani. (After I returned home, I studied these stones and other records intensively and came to the conclusion that this Hani was not my great-great grandmother after all.)

I was surprised to find stones with last names that come from other parts of my grandfather's family that I did not know ever lived in Újhely. Obviously, many families and friends in this area of Hungary moved often between villages and intermarried repeatedly. The caretaker also told me that many "Israelites" from neighboring villages were buried here.

The caretaker showed me areas of my family's plots where many stones were fallen face-down, suggesting many of the people I'm looking for may well be in this cemetery, but aren't visible. There were also a number of stones cut or re-faced recently (one with some of the letters upside down, obviously copied wrong by a non-Jewish stonecutter), some referring to the person having died at (or maybe, having survived and returned from) Auschwitz. One stone was inscribed, in English, to "our grandfather and grandmother."

Many of the stones bore the willow tree designs I had photographed on my earlier trip. The ubiquitous tree of the Hungarian wetlands, which grows only by water, inspires a beautiful image that joins the Jewish concept of the tree of life with the Jewish association of water and Torah. The Reichards are Cohanim (possibly a fake, appointed designation, according to family history) and their gravestones bear the symbol of the blessing hands.

When we found the cemetery in 1997, I knew I had to come back, and I did! On my 1997 trip, my overriding research question was, "Who was David Reichard?" I knew him then only as the *sandak* for Alex and Nick. In the archives on that visit, we found his name as a witness at my great-grandparents' wedding. Then we found the cemetery and David Reichard's name on the donation plaque. Later, at home, I noticed that a postcard to their grandmother from Enny, Olga, and Erzsi was addressed "Reichard Davidné," so I realized that Hani Czinner Perlstein had later married David Reichard. And now, in 2004, I had clearly found his grave. I gave the caretaker a donation for the upkeep of the cemetery, full of gratitude. Even though they have modernized the building and taken away the beautiful doorway that is my favorite photograph from my earlier trip—"*Lech B'Shalom,*" go in peace—this was truly a circle-completing experience.

Fortunately for my existence, by 1913, Grandpa had left Sátoraljaújhely, whose entire Jewish population was deported to Auschwitz in 1944, but I feel now that this is my town, and that I am able, in some way, to maintain the memory of the Jewish presence there. In learning to pronounce *Sha-tor-al-y-a-oo-ee-hey-ee*, I've learned much more.

Holocaust Memorial, Sátoraljaújhely Railroad Station, July 2004

Lech B'Shalom, Go In Peace, Sátoraljaújhely Status Quo Cemetery, 1997

Willow tree on gravestone, Sátoraljaújhely Status Quo Cemetery, 2004

Gravestone of David Reichard, Sátoraljaújhely Status Quo Cemetery, 2004

HARMADIK GENÉRACIÓ MAGYAR

Lynn, Balatonfüred, július 2004

> *"Az itthonról elszármazott vagy második -*
> *harmadik generációs külföldön élo*
> *magyar..."*
> *"The artists from home or second and third*
> *generation from abroad-living*
> *Hungarian..."*
>   from *Müertö* (Budapest July 2004 *Art*
>   *Conoisseur* magazine)

Here I am, having grown up
third-generation American. Two grandparents
Litvak, one Galizianer,
one Magyar. My grandfather, born Friedman Miksa
in Sátoraljaújhely (where Kazinczy wrote
and Kossuth rallied for independence),
left me stories, and my mother
has given me the lace
her Hungarian grandfather had given her,
hoping to make her a suitable Hungarian matron.
And here am I, following the stories
and the lace, eating *halasylé* and *gyulas*,
everything with *paprika,*
drinking *a finom bor* and *pálinka.*

Here am I, *harmadik generació magyar,*
not a stranger to this country
of nineteenth-century buildings, domed and yellow-stuccoed,
lace-curtained windows opening
to the sun. Not a stranger
to the vineyards, grapes ripening for wine,
or to the gardens full of apricot and pear trees,

the fields of sunflowers,
forests of chestnut and oak.

Harmadik generáció magyar,
in the market I ask for and receive
harom gombas, three white mushrooms
to cook with gold-and-red paprika,
squash, and shiny purple onion.
At the *posta* I ask for *harom harminc-forint* stamps,
to complete the postage I need
to send three postcards
airmail to America.

My grandfather called his Grandmother
"a big strapping Hungarian woman."
Accent on Hungarian.
Hani Czinner Perlstein Reichard
of Újhely, widow of the billiards champion of Hungary,
later, sister-in-law of the mayor.
100% Hungarian.

On the bus in Budapest
I look at faces, ask myself
who would have turned me in
in 1944. I walk down narrow ghetto streets,
harmadik generáció magyar,
knowing that Enny's husband Pál, whose name
can be found in the *Aranyalbuma*
published to celebrate the service of Jewish officers
in the First World War, was conscripted
into a Labor Battalion, Enny deported
to Auschwitz, then Buchenwald, their son
shot into the Danube. On the lawn next to our villa
stands a monument
to the Hungarian heroes, a soldier
of the Second World War, exhausted

from what duty? My grandfather
made the right choice,
left behind the formal kissing of hands,
and his sister Enny, perhaps, chose wrong.
But still I am here,
third-generation Hungarian,
according to the art review.

KÖSZI, KÖSZI

Lynn, Wendy, Ruth, 1997 and forever

The one word we've learned to say
is "Köszönöm," *thank you*
and at every opportunity
we practice. Our hosts repeat it back,
in shorter form, "Köszi, Köszi"
with wide grins and dancing eyes
as they hand us our change
of small shiny coins, our packages
of paprika, our velvet vests,
the blue and white candlesticks
carefully wrapped in bubbled plastic.

"Köszi, Köszi" we say to the young boy,
excited to practice his English,
who shows us on the map
that my grandfather's house is too far down the road
to walk, we should take the bus.
The old woman who hangs out the window above us
confers with him, grins at his accomplishment
and at ours. "Köszönöm," we say to her,
and she smiles even wider, "Köszi, Köszi."

FAMILY TREE

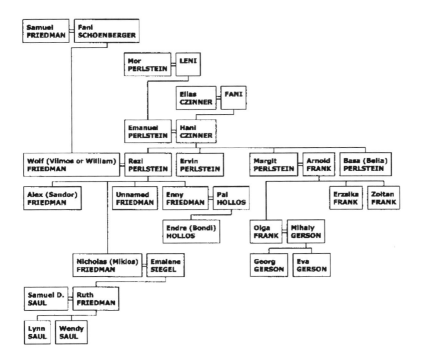

MAP OF HUNGARY, showing places mentioned in this book

SOME EXPLANATIONS

Hungarian names have been presented using the Hungarian practice of giving the family name first (Friedman Samuel) except where Americans are speaking about people using American practice. Married women in Hungary are identified by their husband's names followed by the suffix "-né," with their own maiden name sometimes given in parentheses. Thus, "Dr. Hollós Pálné (Friedman Enny)" is "Mrs. Pál Hollós (including her husband's title of "Dr."), maiden name Enny Friedman." ("Dr." in Hungarian practice includes anyone with a professional degree, not just medical doctors.)

Some inconsistencies in spelling of names (Friedman, Friedmann) are the result of inconsistent practice among the people using those names themselves. (Concern with exact spelling is a relatively recent phenomenon.)

Some inconsistencies between stories occur because I heard different "facts" at different times; my research has sometimes proven oral history to have been wrong or misleading. However, in most cases, I retained the details in stories, poems, and memoir as I wrote them originally.

Jakab Schlanger and David Reichard were both witnesses to the marriage of Wolf Friedman and Rezi Perlstein; fathers commonly take that role, which supports the idea that Jakab Schlanger had married the widowed Fani Friedman and David Reichard had married the widowed Hani Perlstein. David Reichard was also the *sandak* at the bris of Sandor and that of Miksa, an honor traditionally given to the child's grandfather.

In the poetry and fiction in this collection, real people's names are used (along with a few invented characters), historical events are real, but personal stories and characters' inner thoughts are solely imaginative. In the personal essays included ("Cattle Killing I and II," "Learning to Say 'Satoraljaujhely,'" and "The Family and the Holocaust," as well as in other references to "Lynn," the content is non-fiction.

THE FAMILY AND THE HOLOCAUST

When I was growing up, I heard that my grandfather's sister Enny had been at Thereisenstadt during the war. I heard of it as a concentration camp, sometimes as a work camp. I can't remember if I heard that her husband was there too, or not. I knew that she had been there and that she had survived.

I heard, too, that she had brought her son Bondi here to America, and that upon their return to Hungary, generally regarded in the family as a stupid decision on their part, he got off the train and was shot by the Nazis.

Before anyone in America, in the Jewish community in America, was talking about the Holocaust, I knew these facts about my grandfather's family. I knew that my grandfather received letters from his sister, and he told us about their contents.

Later I heard that Thereisenstadt was the German name and that now it is more commonly referred to by its Czech name, Terezin. I learned that it was a "model camp" that the Germans used to confuse the International Red Cross. I read about it, read *I Never Saw a Butterfly*, volunteered as a docent for an exhibit on children's art from Terezin. At the exhibit, I stared at the photographs of the shiny white tile walls and porcelain sinks, at the narrow streets and dark brick walls of the fortress town, at the filmed images of the children's orchestra, young players who would be sent to Auschwitz the next day.

My mother wrote to the Red Cross for information on Enny. Four years later she received a letter, identifying Enny's prisoner number at Auschwitz and Buchenwald, the date of her liberation, a copy of her train ticket home. And the copies of court documents her husband had filed to save her Cegléd and Budapest real estate.

We read about the Hungarian Holocaust. We watched Stephen Spielberg's movie, *The Last Days*. It doesn't seem likely that Bondi was shot on his return from America. It seems more likely that he was part of the underground. Suddenly my mother started to tell a story in which he and his friends "got guns and got into a shootout with the Nazis."

I wrote a story, "The Tablecloth," in which Enny is in Terezin, as is her husband Pál. She is told by another inmate that she has seen Pál, who is quite tall, marching out to work.

Later, when I had proof that Enny was in Auschwitz and Buchenwald, I wrote those places into stories and poems. (Of course, it is possible that Enny was first at Terezin and was later moved to Auschwitz and Buchenwald; these moves did happen to many Hungarians.)

What is the truth? Does it matter? Should I change the facts in "The Tablecloth"? I don't want to, because that story is its own truth. If it didn't happen to Enny Friedman Hollós, it happened to someone else. Maybe even someone Enny knew. And the key facts in "The Tablecloth" are the facts about the tablecloth in Enny's dream. And if they didn't happen to Enny Friedman Hollós, they happened to someone else, whose banquet tablecloth and oversized napkins disappeared into the hands of American soldiers on The Gold Train. The truth is that Enny's niece Ruthie and her sister-in-law Sadie had identical banquet tablecloths and oversized napkins, gifts before the war from Enny's father William. The truth is that I have seen those tablecloths, and I know what Enny's looked like. I have eaten at that table.

Sandor Friedman, Miklos Friedman, Fani Schoenberger Friedman Schlanger, Enny Friedman, Wolf Friedman. Approx. 1910.

Lynn Saul

is a poet and writer whose work has been published in a number of literary magazines and anthologies. She has also published several chapbooks of poetry, including *I am Trying to Understand*, an earlier version of some of the material in this book. Her MFA in creative writing was earned at the University of Arizona.

After a long career as an attorney, including eight years as a legal services lawyer on the Tohono O'Odham Nation in southern Arizona, Saul retired from the practice of law to focus exclusively on writing and teaching. She teaches writing and humanities at Pima Community College in Tucson, Arizona. She also leads community and synagogue writing workshops.

Saul is an avid gardener, an interest that obviously traces back at least as far as her great-great-grandparents in Hungary.

6220826R0

Made in the USA
Charleston, SC
28 September 2010